MR. PRESIDENT Goes to School

Written by RICK WALTON

Illustrated by BRAD SNEED

PEACHTREE
ATLANTA

Mr. President was having a crummy day.

The National Gopher Society was demanding that gophers be allowed in the Rose Garden. "Gophers?" cried the White House gardener. "Why, they'll turn my lawn into Swiss cheese!"

Then there was the problem of the
Ping-Pong table.
Mr. President loved playing Ping-Pong.
But Mr. Vice President had told a visiting
troop of Boy Scouts they could chop it up
for their marshmallow roast.
Finally, there was that call from
Madam Secretary of State.

MR. P.

MR. V.P.

"Mr. President," said Madam Secretary. "Bulrovia is threatening to go to war with Snortburg—and vice versa! It's the Sticks and Stones issue, again, sir. What should we do?"

Not another war.

"I don't know," Mr. President sighed. He hung up the phone and sat thinking of a happier time and a happier place.

Then he smiled. He pulled a long coat from his closet, tucked his head under a large floppy hat, and put on a fake nose and glasses from an old spy kit.

He slipped out of the big white house and walked exactly seven and a half blocks...

...to a place where the world was a little simpler.

"Well, well! Who do we have here?" asked the white-haired lady. "A new student?"

Mr. President smiled and nodded.

"My name is Mrs. Appletree," said the lady. "What's yours?"

"Louis," said Mr. President.

"Such a nice name. I had a student named Louis once. He's an important man now."

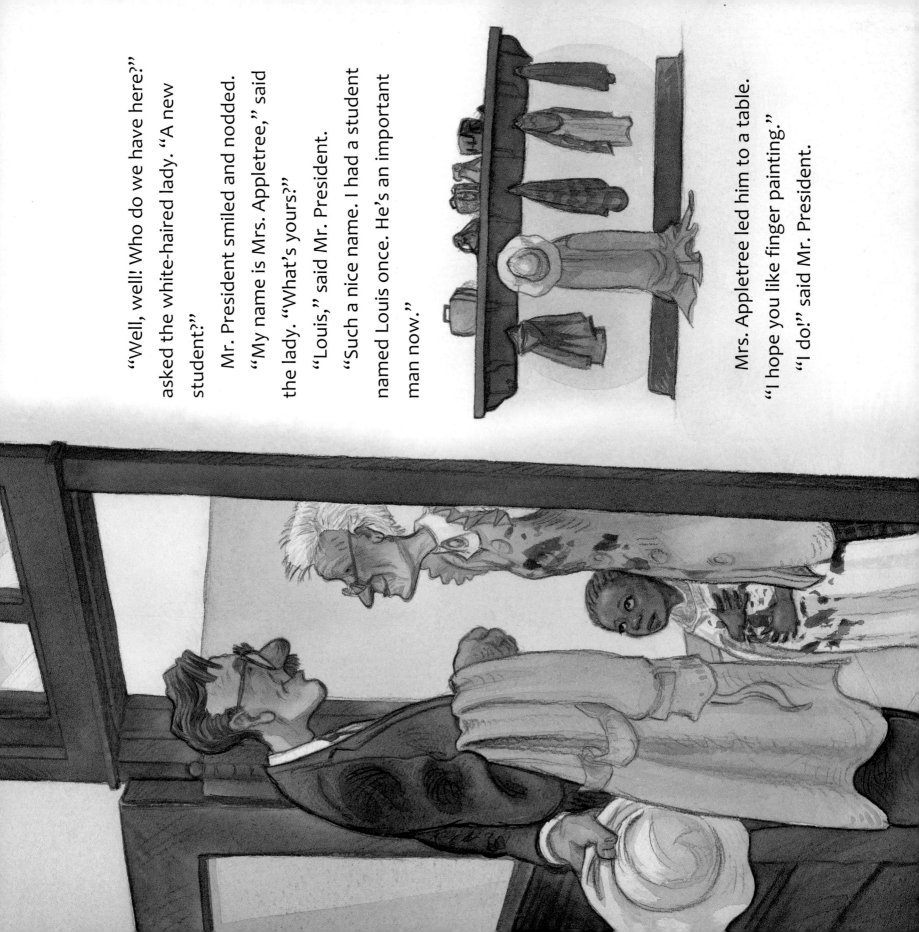

Mrs. Appletree led him to a table. "I hope you like finger painting."

"I do!" said Mr. President.

He slid his fingers through the globs of green paint.

"That's very pretty, Louis," said Mrs. Appletree. "What is it?"

"A Ping-Pong table," said Mr. President.

He was feeling better already.

After finger painting, it was time for recess.

Mr. President made two friends,

chased a squirrel,

and spun himself silly.

Back inside, he and his new friends made a castle out of blocks. "I get to be king!" everyone shouted.

"Come now, we're all friends here," Mrs. Appletree said.
"Friends can always work things out. But I'll bet you're hungry.
It's hard to solve problems when you're hungry."
Mrs. Appletree passed out milk and cookies. And soon,
with full tummies, everyone lay down for a nap.

When they woke up, it was storytime.
Everyone sat crisscross applesauce on
the carpet and Mrs. Appletree began to
read. Several times she stopped and asked
questions. "But raise your hands," she
would say. "Polite people always raise
their hands."

Mr. President raised his hand.
He answered three questions.
Two of them correctly.

"Our day is almost over," said Mrs. Appletree.

"What very important thing do we still need to do?"

"The hokey pokey!" the children shouted.

They put their right legs in.
They put their right legs out.
They put their left arms in.
They put their left arms out.

And they shook it all about
until the bell rang.

Mr. President laughed. "I love
the hokey pokey!"
"Yes, Louis," said Mrs. Appletree.
"That's what it's all about."

Mr. President skipped all the
way back to the White House.

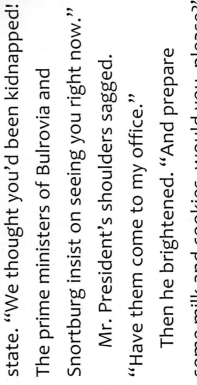

"THERE you are!" cried the secretary of state. "We thought you'd been kidnapped! The prime ministers of Bulrovia and Snortburg insist on seeing you right now."

Mr. President's shoulders sagged.

"Have them come to my office."

Then he brightened. "And prepare some milk and cookies, would you, please?"

Polite people always say please.

Mr. President sat on the big oval rug and waited. The two leaders were horrified. Prime ministers sit in grand chairs, not on carpets. And especially not crisscross applesauce. They looked at each other and frowned.

Mr. President patted the rug. "Please, sit down. We're all friends here."

Each man lowered himself to the floor.

"Well then," said Mr. President, "I hear we have a problem."

The angry prime ministers began to shout.

INCOMPOOP!! NINNY!

"Now, now," said Mr. President. "Before we speak, we do what?" The two leaders looked puzzled.

"We raise our hands," said Mr. President. The prime minister of Bulrovia slowly raised his hand.

"Yes?" said Mr. President.

"THEY are throwing sticks across the river at us!"

"YOU are throwing stones at US, you doofus!" the prime minister of Snortburg snarled.

"Oh dear, there's that name-calling again," said Mr. President. "But I know what may help."

Mr. President asked Madam Secretary to serve the milk and cookies.

When all the cookies were gone, the prime ministers yawned. "It's hard to solve problems when we're sleepy," said Mr. President.

His new friends nodded. At last, they'd found something they could agree on.

After they awoke, Mr. President said, "Now, there is something important we must do. The hokey pokey!"

The two leaders shook their heads. Prime ministers DO NOT do the hokey pokey.

"Try it once," said Mr. President.

They put their left arms in.
They put their left arms out.
They put their backsides in.
They put their backsides out.

The second time around, the prime minister of Bulrovia really shook it all about, which made the prime minister of Snortburg laugh.

"That was fun," he said. "Can we play another game?"

"Sure!" said Mr. President. "Let's build a castle. We can take turns being king."

Finally, Mr. President had the White House chef
mix up some finger paints, and they all drew pictures.
There wasn't a stick or a stone in any of them.

"Now," Mr. President asked, "what were
you two arguing about?"

The two prime ministers stopped painting.
For an awful moment no one spoke. Then the
prime minister of Snortburg did a very brave
thing. "Surely we can work SOMETHING out,"
he said. "We're all friends here."

The prime minister of Bulrovia looked at
him and smiled.

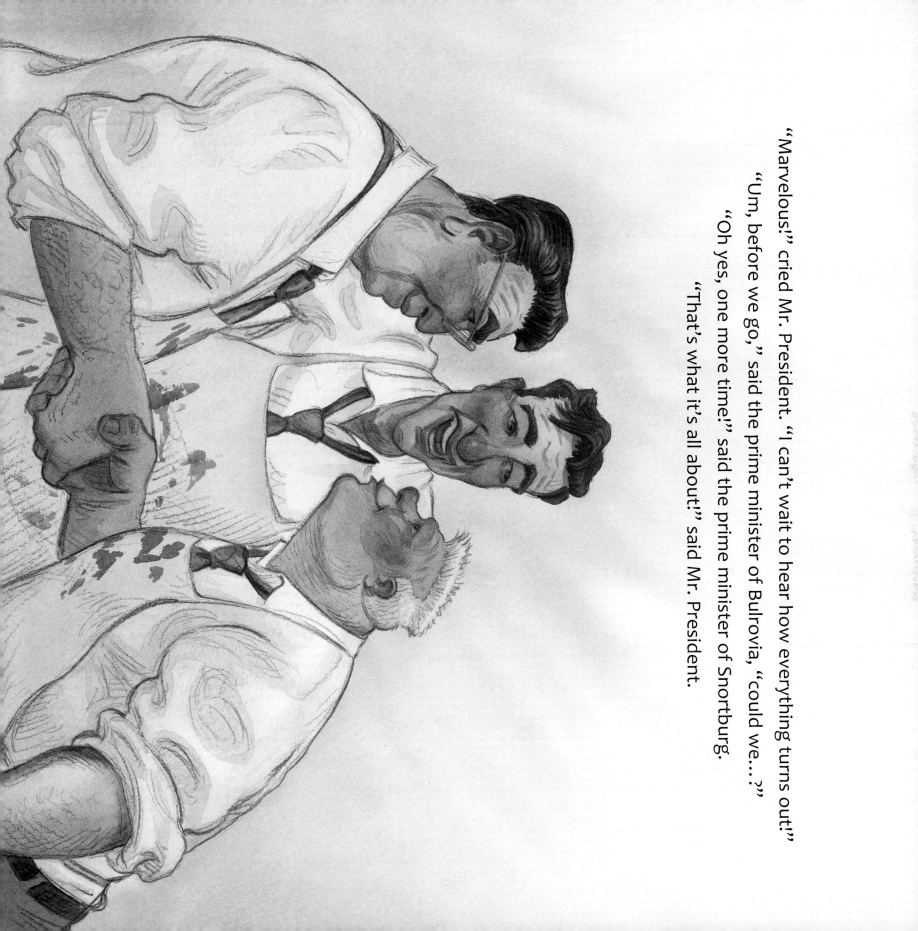

"Marvelous!" cried Mr. President. "I can't wait to hear how everything turns out!"

"Um, before we go," said the prime minister of Bulrovia, "could we...?"

"Oh yes, one more time!" said the prime minister of Snortburg.

"That's what it's all about!" said Mr. President.

The next morning Mr. President looked out his office window and sighed.

He pulled a long coat from his closet,
tucked his head under a large floppy hat, and
put on the fake nose and glasses he had found
in an old spy kit.
Then he slipped out of the big white house
and walked to a place exactly seven and
a half blocks away...

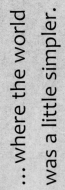

...where the world
was a little simpler.

To my parents, Bill and Wilma Walton,
who taught me what it's all about.

—R. W.

In memory of my grandpa, Glenn Johnson,
a gentle soul.

—B. S.

Published by
PEACHTREE PUBLISHERS
1700 Chattahoochee Avenue
Atlanta, Georgia 30318-2112

www.peachtree-online.com

Text © 2010 by Rick Walton
Illustrations © 2010 by Brad Sneed

Acquired by Carmen Agra Deedy
Art direction by Loraine M. Joyner
Illustrations created in watercolor and colored pencil on cold press watercolor paper. Title typeset in Fontalicious's P. S. Academy and Kix's ariapencilroman; text typeset in Microsoft's Candara by Gary Munch.

Words from "The Hokey Pokey" used by permission. Copyright 1950 Sony/ATV Music Publishing LLC. All rights administered by Sony/ATV Music Publishing LLC, Nashville, Tennessee. All rights reserved.

Printed and manufactured in March 2010 by Imago in Singapore
10 9 8 7 6 5 4 3 2 1

First Edition

Library of Congress Cataloging-in-Publication Data

Walton, Rick.
Mr. President goes to school / written by Rick Walton ; illustrated by Brad Sneed.
   p. cm.
Summary: When the President finds the many pressures of his job to be overwhelming, he disguises himself and returns to kindergarten, where he is reminded of the important lessons he learned there.
ISBN 13: 978-1-56145-538-6 ISBN 10: 1-56145-538-5
[1. Kindergarten—Fiction. 2. Schools—Fiction. 3. Presidents—Fiction. 4. Humorous stories.] I. Sneed, Brad, ill. II. Title. III. Title: Mister President goes to school.
PZ7.W1774Mr 2010
[E]—dc22

2009040352